T5-ACQ-502

At last Mop was home. And that was where he wanted to stay.

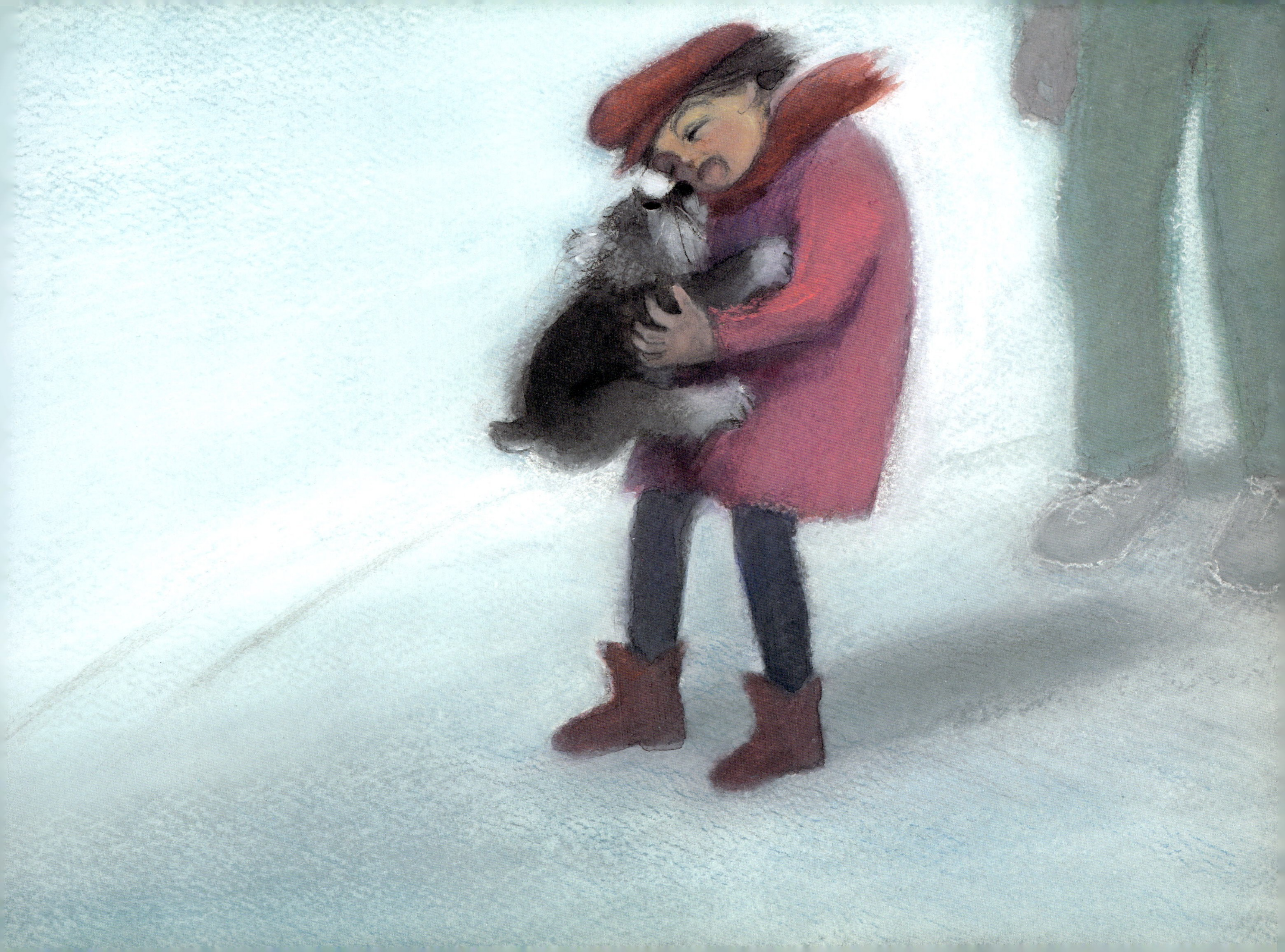

Michan rang the bell and waited nervously on the doorstep. What if it wasn't Mop?

Just then a man came to the door, and before Michan could say anything, a furry ball bounced out from behind the man's legs and into Michan's arms.

"Oh, Mop! It really *is* you!"

Michan thanked the kind people and hugged her lost-and-found friend tightly so he couldn't get lost—again.

The next day, Michan was putting a "lost" sign on a telephone pole, when her neighbor called to her.
   "Michan! Michan! I saw a picture that looks just like Mop!"
   "Where?" Michan felt breathless.
   "I'll show you."
   Michan hoped and hoped that it really was Mop. She hurried after her neighbor, and finally they stood in front of a large house on Fifth Street.

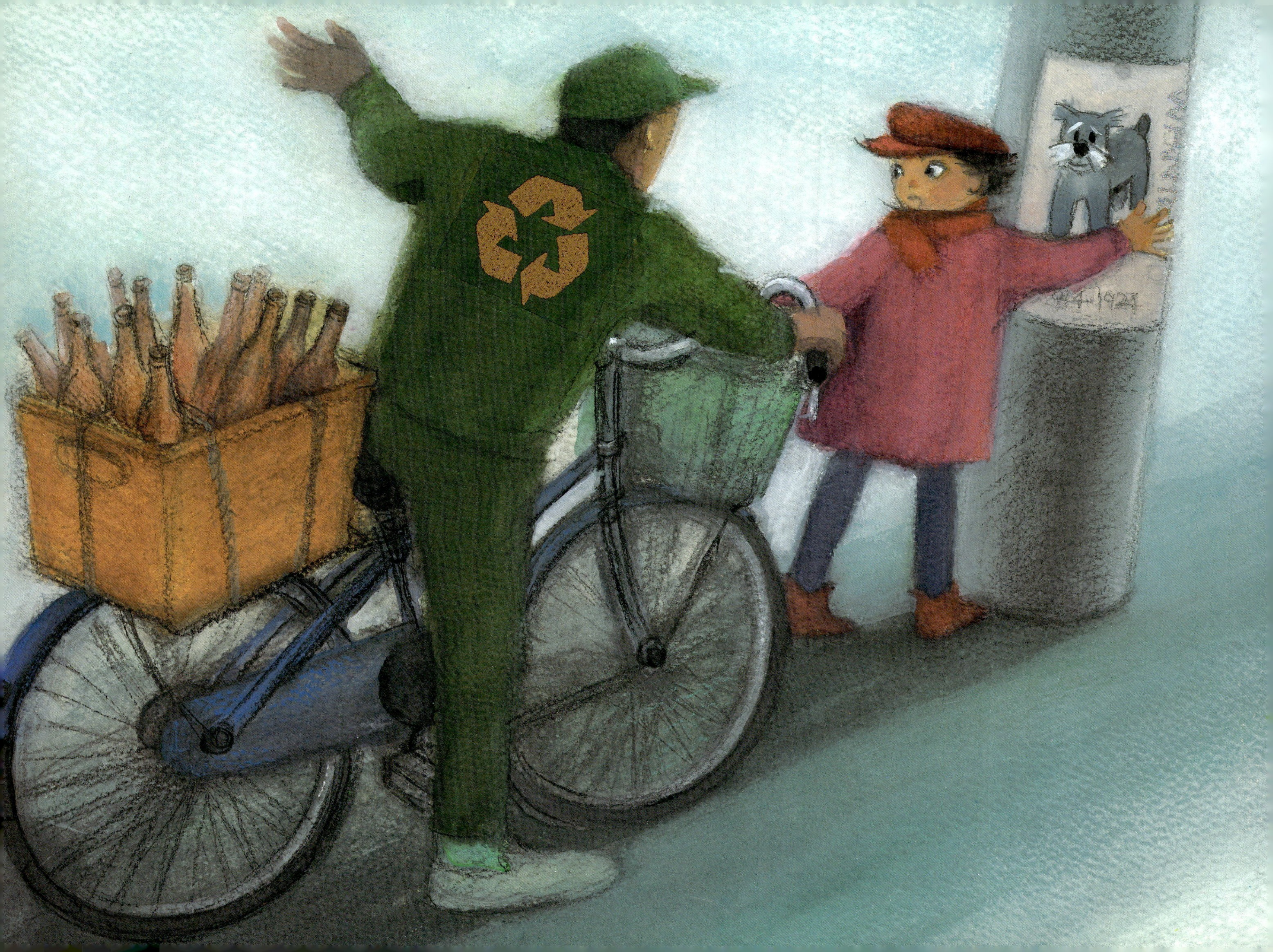

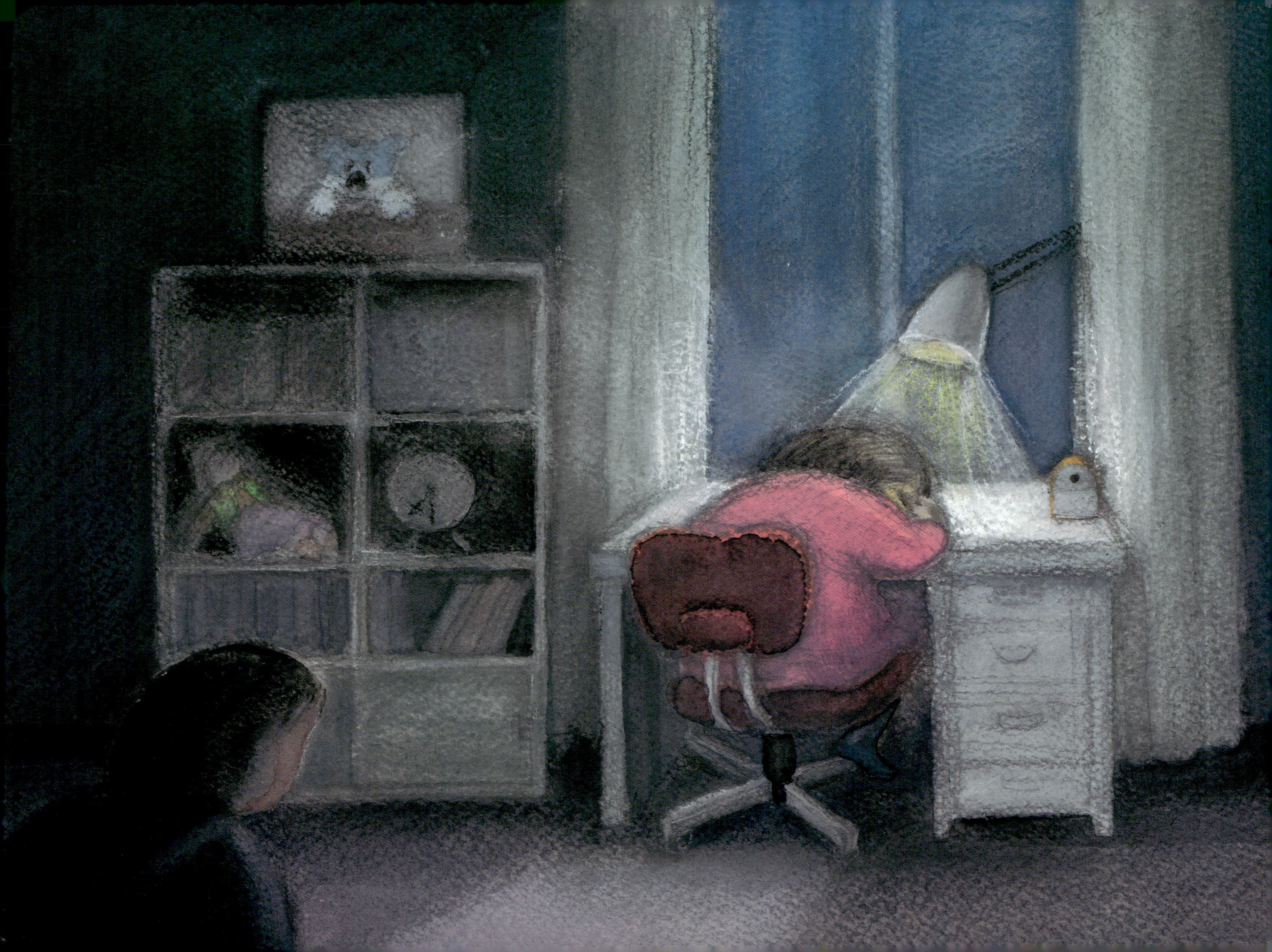

Mop had been missing for a whole week.
All this time, Michan could do nothing but think of Mop and cry.
She didn't know where to look for her little lost dog.
Michan's mother was worried about her. "Why don't you get some people to help you look for Mop," she suggested.

PUPPY FOUND!!

If he is yours, come to
1017 East Fifth Street

On his way home from work the next day, the man hung posters on buildings near his house. They had a picture of Mop on them.

The man took Mop home with him. He and his wife gave Mop water and something to eat.
"There you are. Eat as much as you like," he said.
But Mop was tired and sad. He didn't feel like eating. Mop missed Michan.

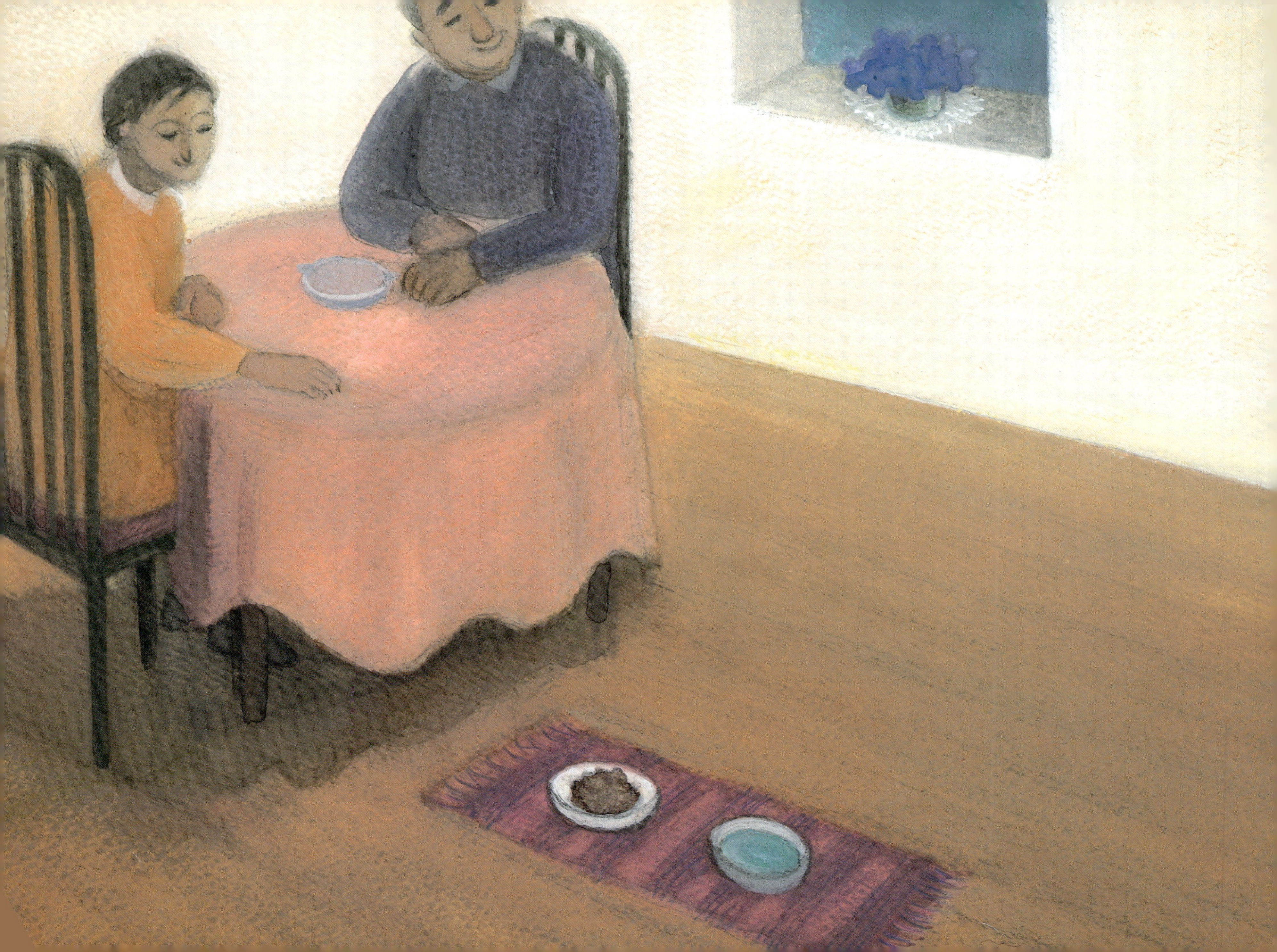

A blue car slowed down, and a man stuck his head out the window. "Are you lost little feller?" the man asked. "If you play in a place like this, you'll get run over, you know. Why don't you hop in our car."
He opened the door for Mop.

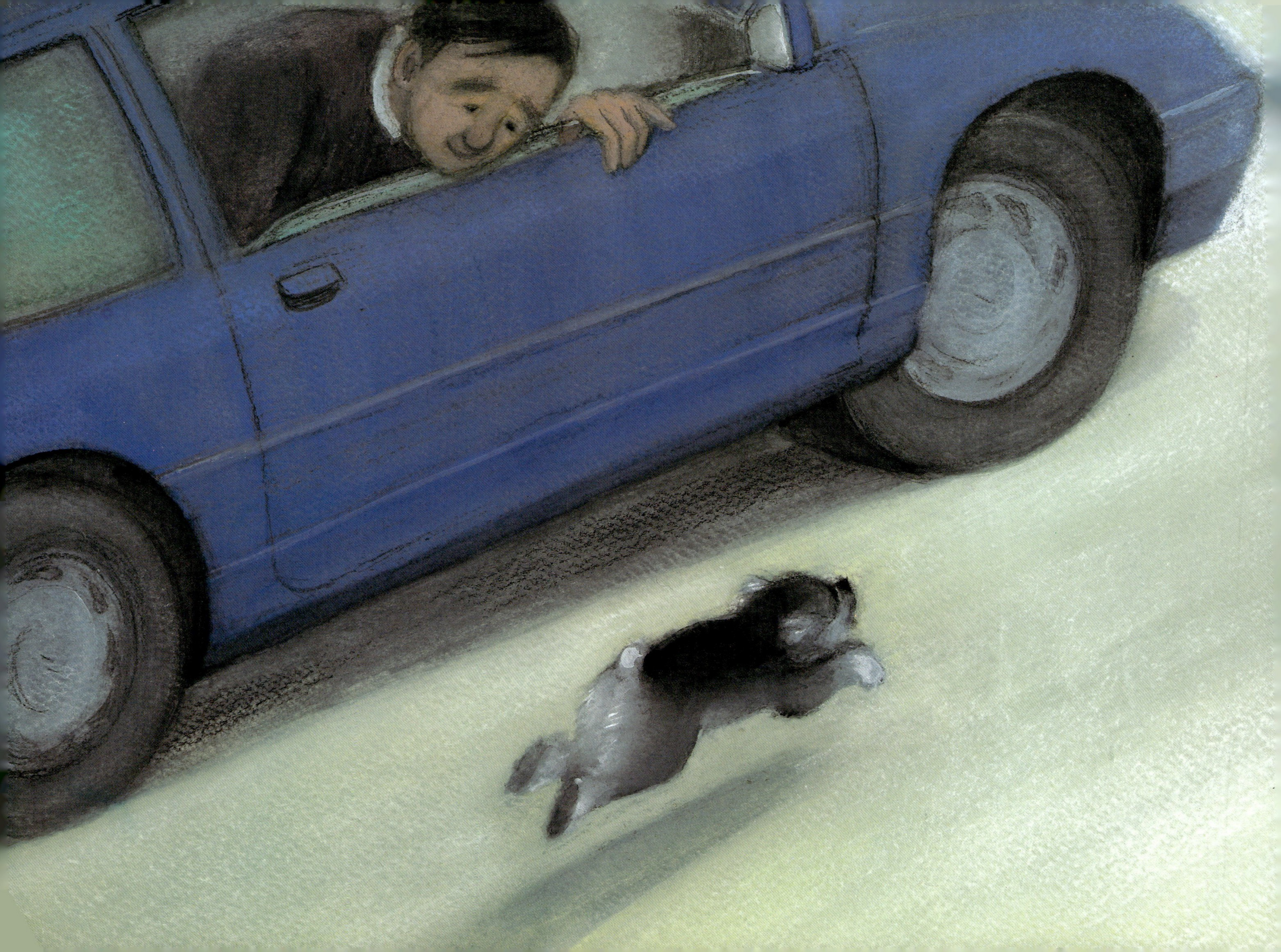

Was he getting closer or farther away from Michan?
Maybe these cars knew the way.

He came to a road crowded with speeding cars and raced along beside them.

The van carrying the white dog got smaller and smaller until it disappeared.

I sure hope Michan's looking for me, Mop thought. I better look for her, too. But he didn't know where he was or where to look.

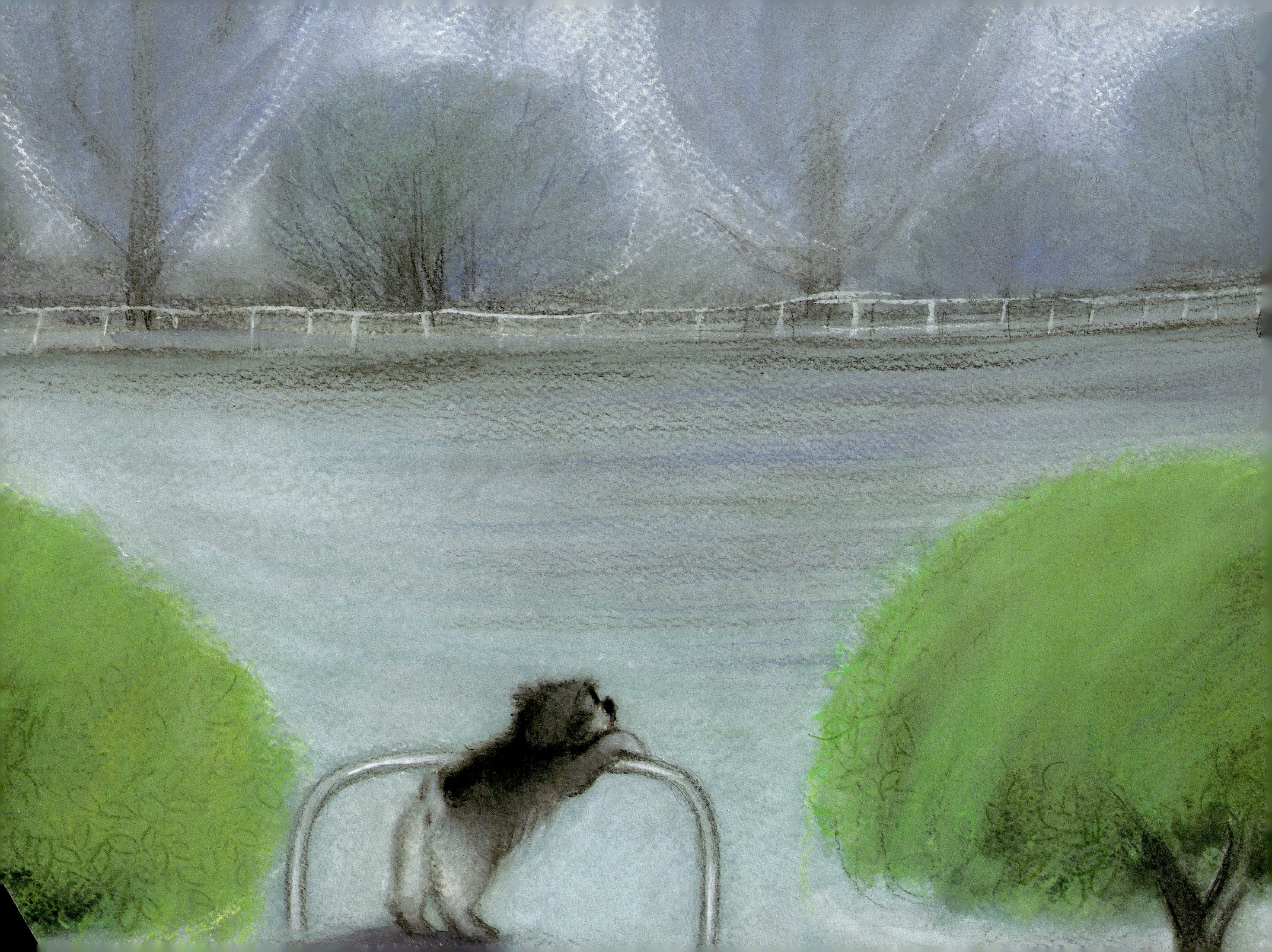

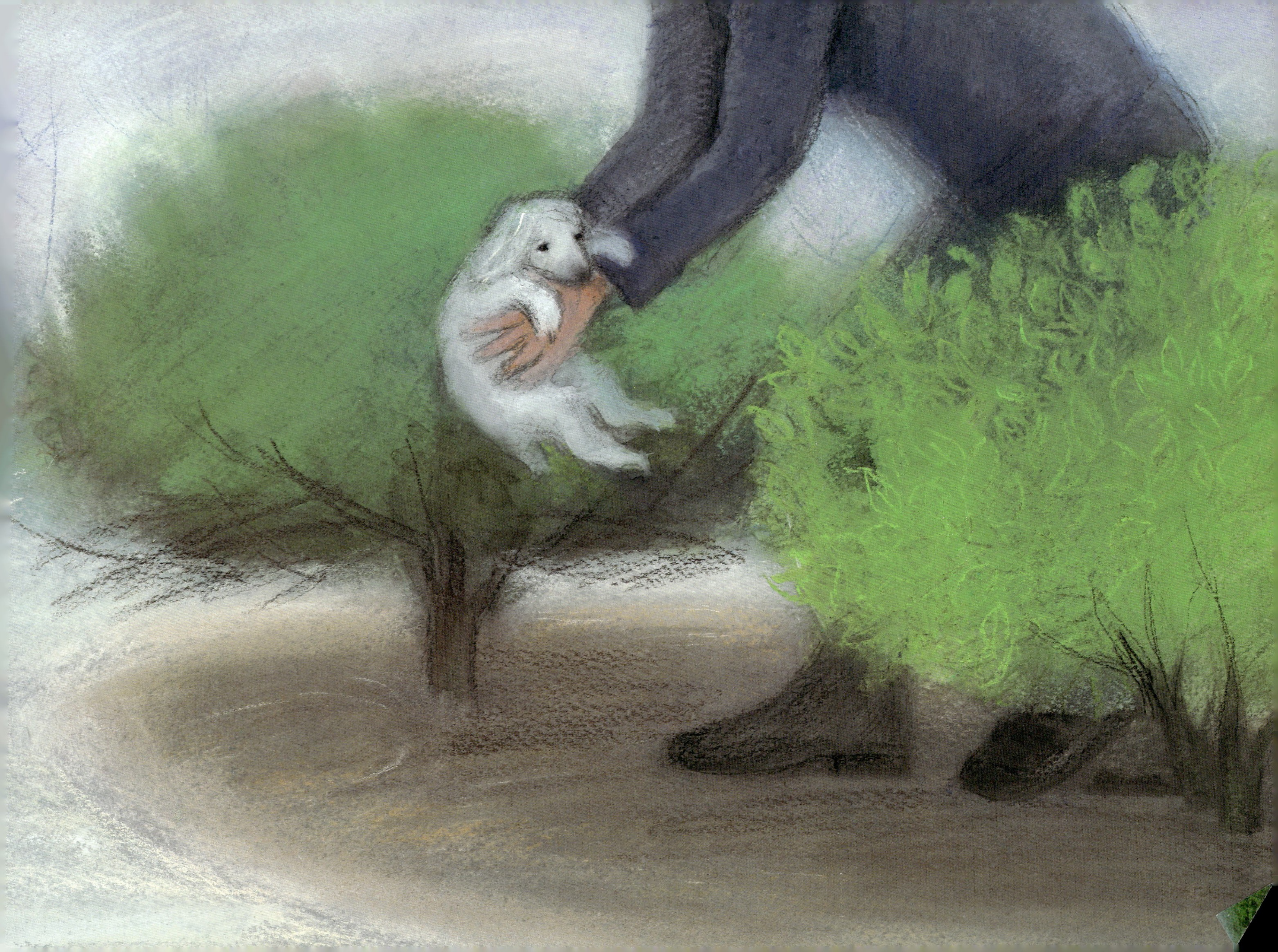

In the morning, Mop went looking for food for them.
   He came back just in time to see a man picking up the white dog. He knew that man. He was from the pound. Michan had told Mop that the pound takes homeless animals off the streets.
   Mop was scared. He stayed as still as he could in the bushes. Mop *did* have a home—and he wanted to find it before anyone took *him* to the pound.

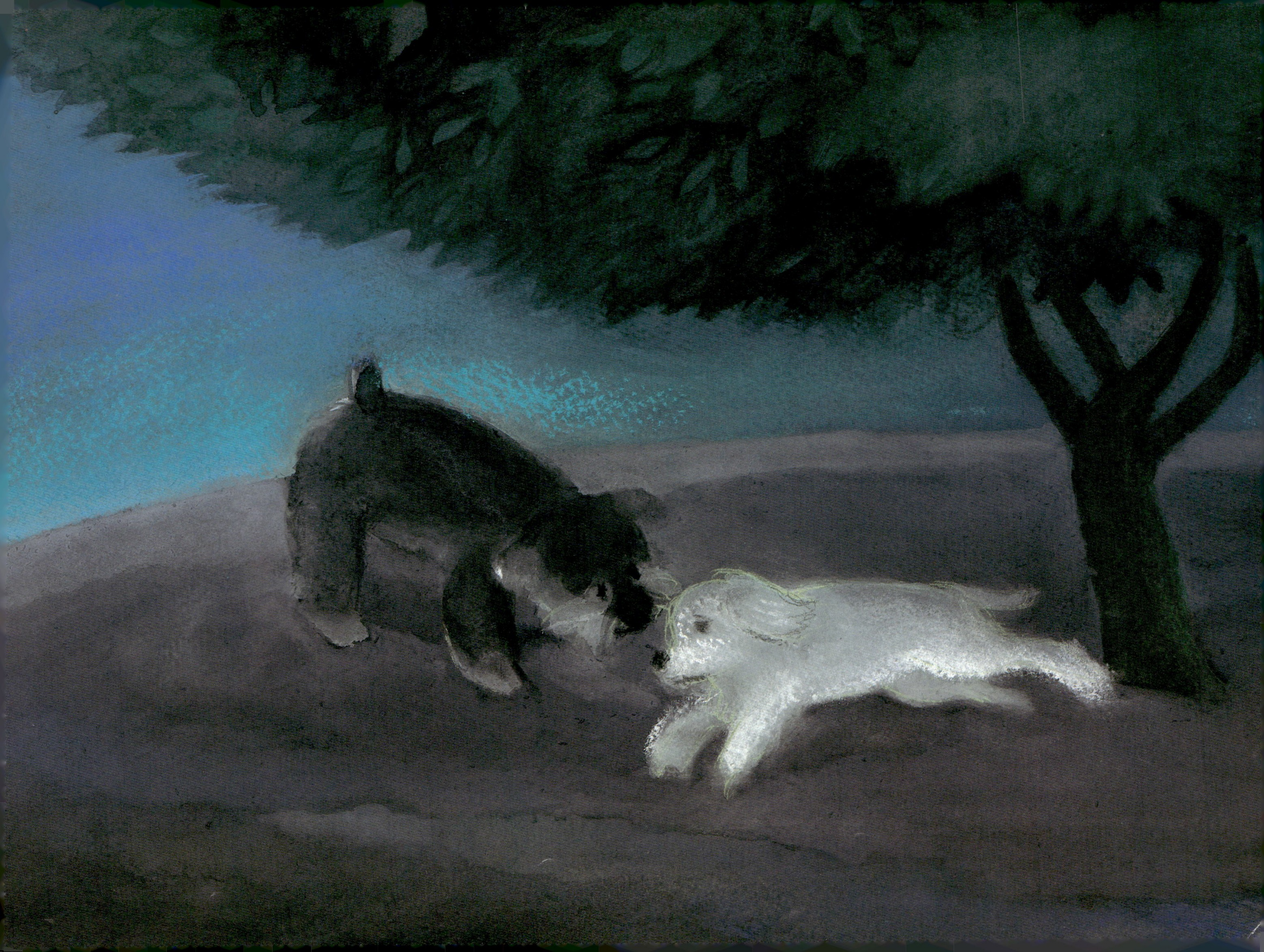

Mop followed the sound and found a small white dog lying in the grass.
    Mop wagged his tail hello.
    The white dog whimpered sadly. He told Mop that he was waiting for his owner. She had dropped him off and had not come back— and that had been days ago.
    Mop lay down next to him, and the two lonely dogs spent the night sleeping close together.

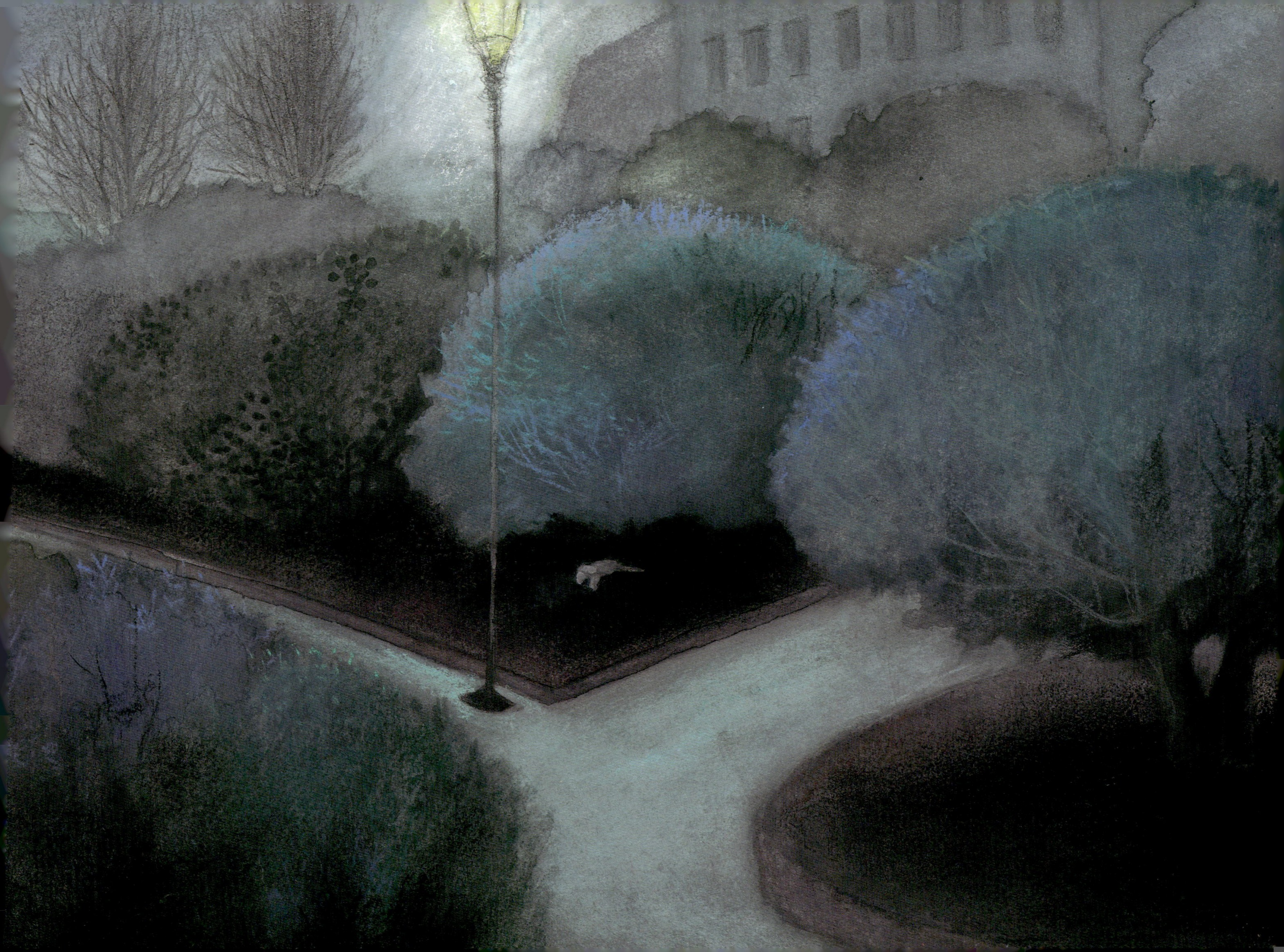

When he finally stopped running, Mop was in a park he'd never seen before.
Where am I? Where's Michan?
It was getting dark, and Mop felt very alone.
Mop was lost.
From under some trees, he heard a faint whimper.

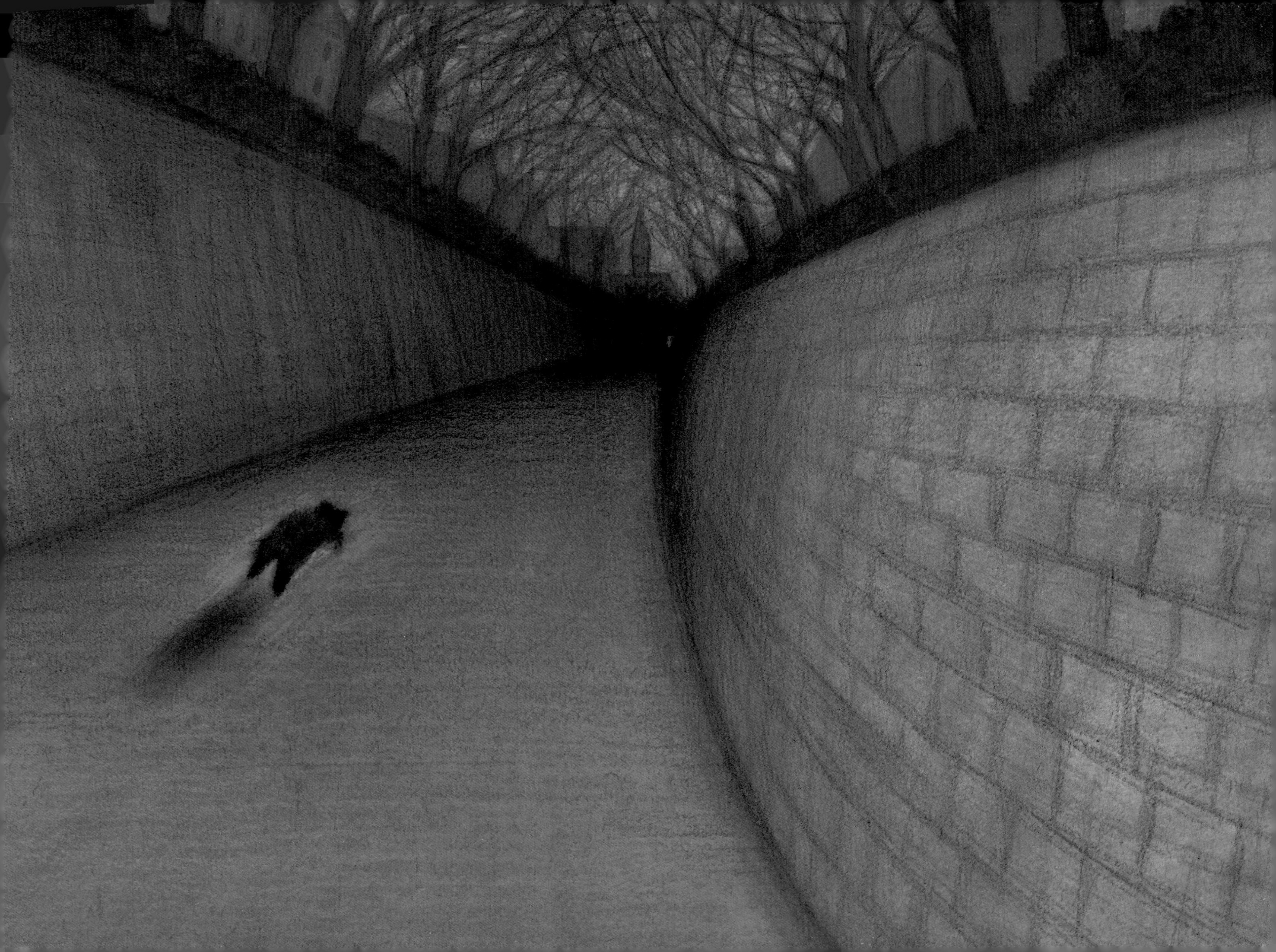

TKK-TKK-TKK-TKK
The terrible noise seemed to follow him.
Mop raced away as fast as he could.

TKK-TKK-TKK-TKK-TKK
　　Suddenly the whole street shook with the sound of a jackhammer. Red lights and red cones were everywhere—but where were Michan's red boots?
　　Mop was terrified! He started to run.

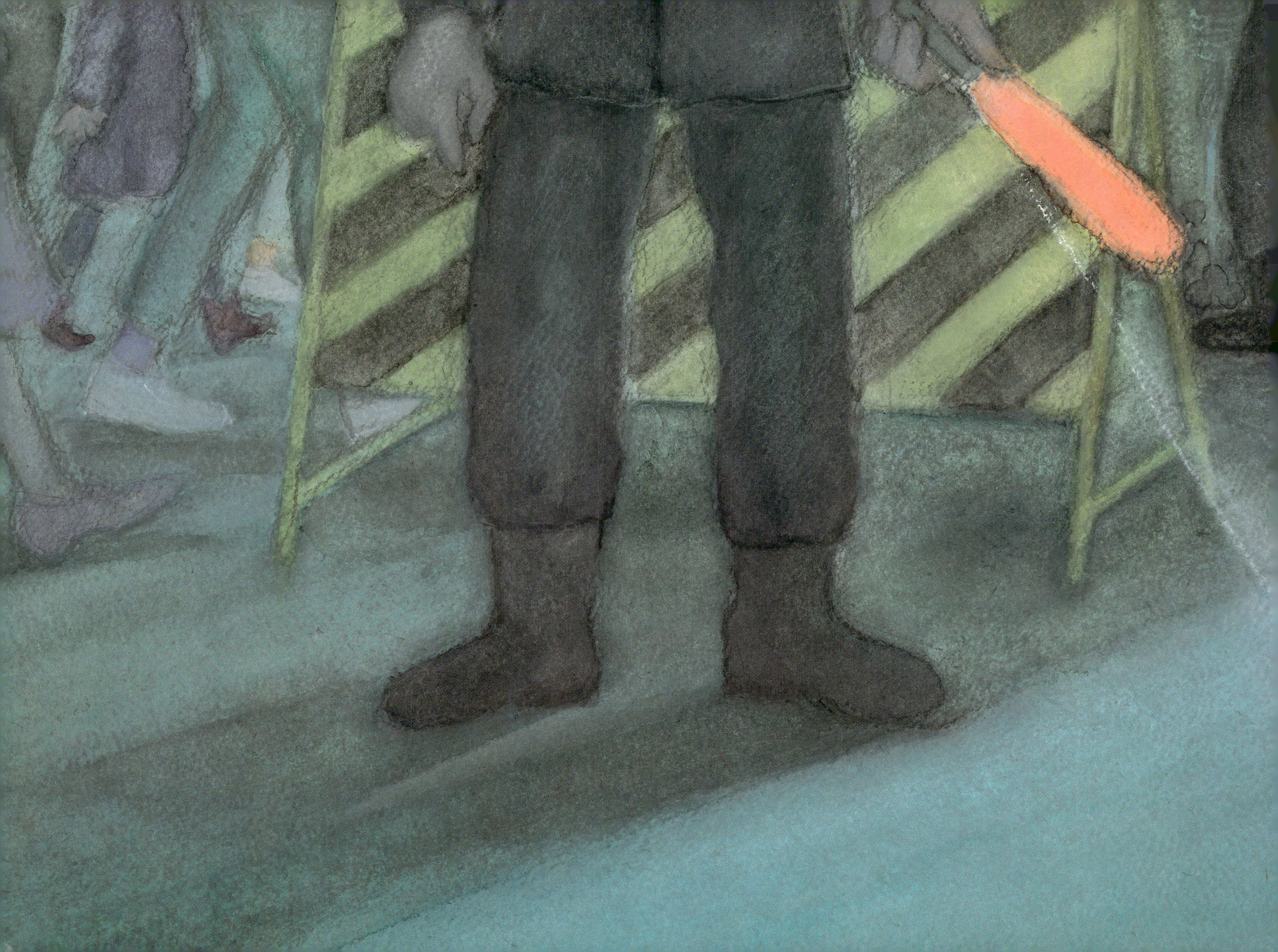

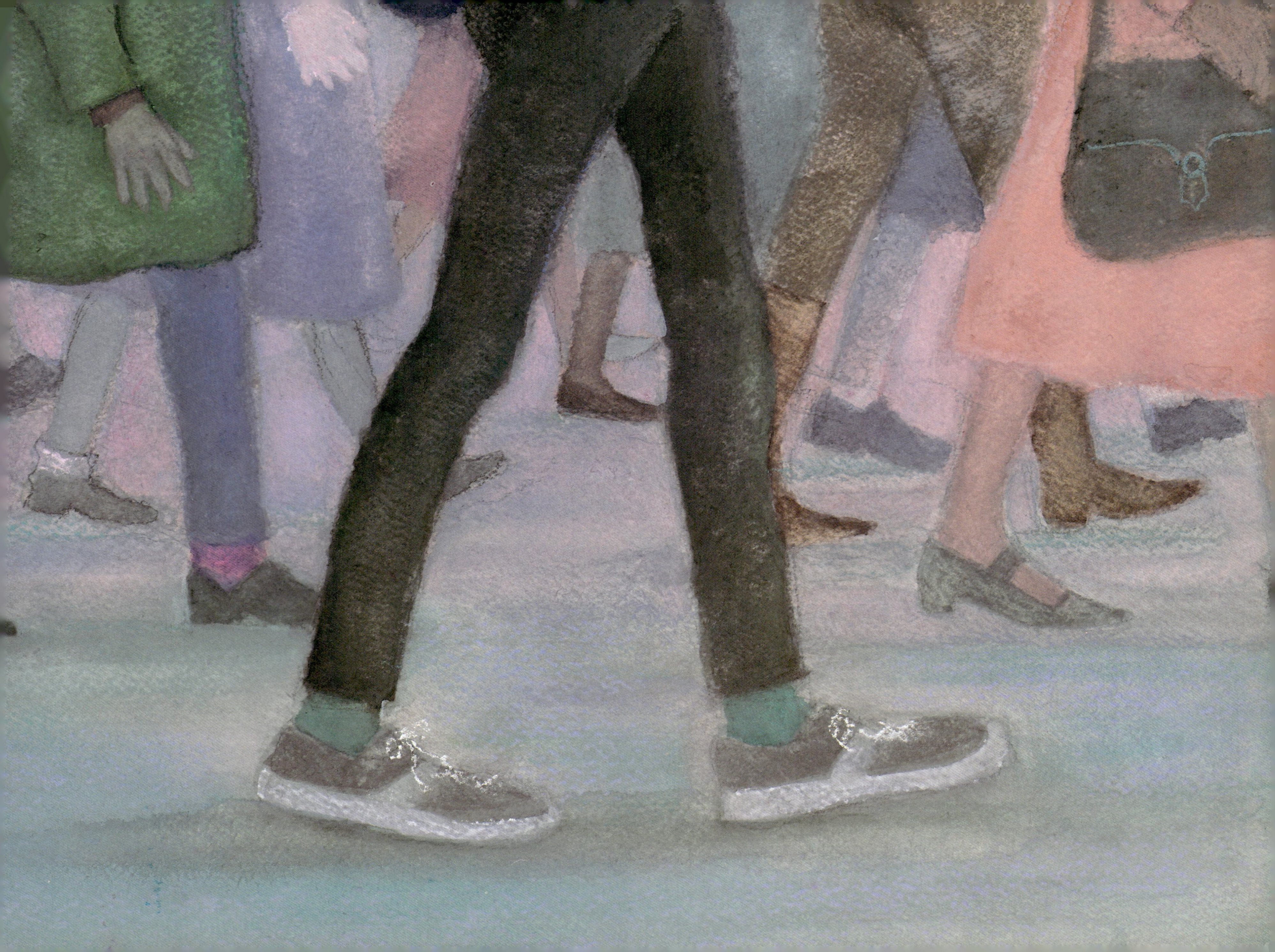

Just as they passed the train station, a train pulled in.
People crowded into the streets.
Mop tried hard to keep up with Michan's red boots.

"Hey, Mop! Let's go for a walk," called Michan when she came home from school.
Mop bounced after her.
Mop loved his walks with Michan.

This edition first published 1992 by Carolrhoda Books, Inc.

First published in Japan in 1989 by Fukutake Publishing Co. under the title MAIGO NI NATTA MOP.
Copyright © 1989 by Kayoko Kanome.
Translated from the Japanese by Prudence Moodie.

All rights to this edition reserved by Carolrhoda Books, Inc. No part of this book may be reproduced, stored in a retrieval system, or transmitted in any form or by any means, electronic, mechanical, photocopying, recording, or otherwise, without the prior written permission of the Publisher except for the inclusion of brief quotations in an acknowledged review.

Library of Congress Cataloging-in-Publication Data

Kanome, Kayoko.
  [Maigo ni natta Mop. English]
  Little Mop lost / Kayoko Kanome.
    p.   cm.
  Translation of: Maigo ni natta Mop.
  Summary: A little girl takes her dog, Mop, for a walk but when they become separated by traffic, Mop gets lost.
  ISBN 0-87614-738-4
  [1. Dogs—Fiction. 2. City and town life—Fiction.] I. Title.
PZ7.K1175Li 1992
[E]—dc20
                                  91-43996
                                      CIP
                                      AC

Manufactured in the United States of America
1 2 3 4 5 6 7 8 9 10 01 00 99 98 97 96 95 94 93 92

Little Mop Lost

by Kayoko Kanome

Carolrhoda Books, Inc./Minneapolis